Alice the Fairy

Alice the Fairy

David Shannon

SCHOLASTIC INC.
New York Toronto London Auckland Sydney
Mexico City New Delhi Hong Kong Buenos Aires

To Emma the Fairy
and the lovely Duchess
(who isn't really wicked at all)

This book was originally published in hardcover by the Blue Sky Press in 2004.

ISBN 0-439-79165-0

12 11 10 9 8 9 10/0

Printed in the U.S.A. 40

First Scholastic paperback printing, September 2005

My name is Alice. I'm a fairy!

I'm not a Permanent fairy. I'm a Temporary fairy. You have to pass alot of tests to be a Permanent fairy.

I have wings so I can fly!

I can't fly very high yet,

but I can fly
really fast!

This is my magic wand.

This is my blanket.

Fairies use magic wands to change frogs into princes and things like that.

I changed my dad into a horse.

One time my mom made cookies for my dad.

So I turned them into mine.

I felt bad about the cookies, so I thought I'd whip up a new outfit for my dad. Did I tell you he's the Duke of Morningside Drive? Well, he is!

But clothes were too hard, so I made him a new crown instead.

With my magic wand, I can
make leaves fall from trees.

And I can draw pictures on water.

Sometimes I use my wand to disappear.

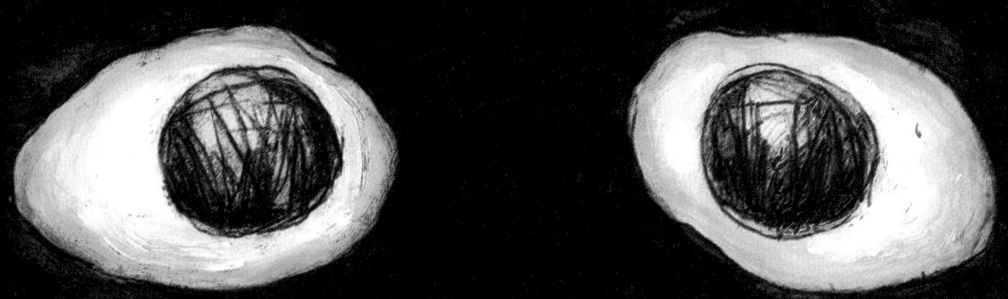

But that's kind of scary.

I'd rather

use my blanket!

Of course, I also have a Magic Mirror.

"Mirror, mirror,
on the wall,
who's the
fairiest of
them all?"

Well, what do you know - it's
me, Alice!
Thank you, Mirror!

Fairy dust is very useful. I use it to turn oatmeal into cake.

Casting spells is another important part of being a fairy. Watch me make my dog float on the ceiling.

Hocus Pocus
croakin Docus!

Howkin Towkin
Riggin Fowlkin!

Doggin Floggin Biddle Noggin!!

Okay... that one needs a little work.

But, a fairy must

be very careful with magic. Once I accidentally turned my white dress into a red one.

That made the Duchess so mad she locked me in the tower forever!

(I got away, though.)

A fairy's life is filled with danger. Broccoli is often poisoned by the wicked Duchess and should <u>never</u> be eaten.

Fairies also hate baths. I'd like to turn my bathwater into Strawberry Jell-O. That would be fun!

But, I don't know how yet.

You have to be a Permanent fairy to do tricks like that.

They go to Advanced Fairy School to learn how.

I'm supposed to learn how to make clothes get up off the floor and dance around and line up in the closet.

I'm not very good at

that, though.

I'll probably be a Temporary fairy forever.